Where the Waters Begin

The Traditional Nisqually Indian History of Mount Rainier

by Cecilia Svinth Carpenter
Indian Historian

*Cover: Native Americans with canoes on beach at Vashon Island with Mount Rainier
in background. A. H. Barnes, 1911. University of Washington Libraries, Special
Collections, BARNES300*

*Back: Glaciers of the southwest slope as viewed from a portion of Indian Henry's Park.
Photo by A.H. Barnes, 1907. University of Washington Libraries Special Collections,
BARNES386 .*

*This Book is Dedicated
To the Memory of My Brother*

*M/SGT Paul W. Svinth
1927-1961*

*Whose Spirit Soars Above the Clouds and Touches the Mountaintop
to Commune With God*

Table of Contents

Spread Out: A representation of a plant that spreads out as a fern does, this Southern Puget Salish design is found on Puyallup and Suquamish works.

From: Crow's Shells: Artistic Basketry of Puget Sound by Nile Thompson and Carolyn Marr

Introduction

Through this writing I am going to take you up the Nisqually side of Mount Rainier and share with you my knowledge as together we climb to that part of the mountain where the trees stop growing and the eternal snowfields lie deep–to that spot marking the sacred demarcation line that encircles the entire mountain. From that vantage point we shall look upward to the three peaks of lofty Tahoma, sacred Ta-co-bet, and I shall tell you why Indian people do not desire to trespass on the holy land that lies above that sacred line.

I shall share with you the beliefs of the traditional Nisqually Indian people who lived in times long past. I shall tell you of the appreciation and fear of this great mountain that my people so greatly respected. I shall relate the historical uses of the natural resources of the lower mountain slopes and identify our foot-hill village areas that were established on the mighty Nisqually River that feeds from its glacier high on the mountainside.

My historical narrative will deal almost entirely with the Nisqually side of the mountain. It is my belief that while I may know of the historical accounts of my neighboring tribes, I cannot speak for them. I speak, therefore, only as one of my people, the Nisqually, whose moccasins have trod the paths up the mountainside in centuries past and whose memories have been passed down through the ages to the generation in which I live. I shall write this account so that my children and grandchildren will look mountainward and not forget. I shall write this account so that you, the reader, will understand why the Nisqually Indian people revere the beautiful mountain we call Ta-co-bet.

Cecelia Svinth Carpenter

2

Basket design much like that of Nisqually baskets. University of Washington Libraries, Special Collections, NA676

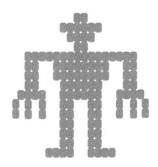

Humans: Southern Puget Salish baskets occasionally contain representations of human figures. Females are distinguished from males on a Nisqually basket by skirts and a smaller waist. On Nisqually and Puyallup examples both feet and hands are depicted. When fingers are shown they number three. On a Puyallup basket four men are standing in a row holding hands waist high. On a Nisqually work the figures are placed randomly in two rows—some with lowered hands, some with raised hands.

From: Crow's Shells: Artistic Basketry of Puget Sound by Nile Thompson and Carolyn Marr

PART ONE: The Nisqually Indian People

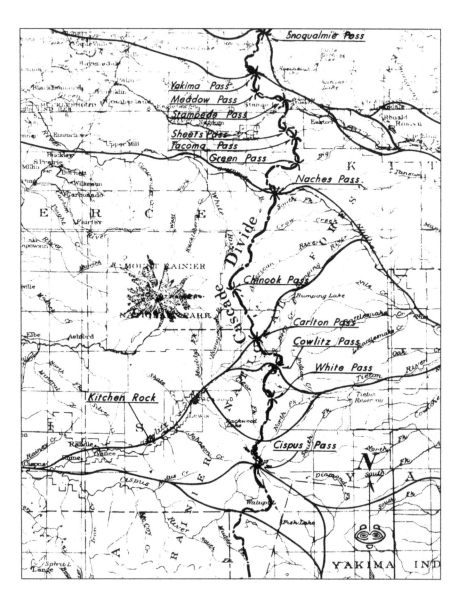

Major trails and passes used by the Indians in crossing the Cascades as of about 1850. From The Washington Archaeologist, Vol. VIII, No. 1, January, 1964.

The People Came – *Chapter 1*

When did the people come to the lands that lay west of Mount Rainier? How many years had passed after the Cascade Mountains pushed up out of the sea before the people came? No one really knows. But it is said that years and years after the earth shook and rocked and growled, the Cascade Mountains appeared out of the bowels of the sea, lining up in a north-south direction, the higher peaks reaching skyward like sentinels with their heads reaching up to the clouds.

After the mountain-building came the blankets of ice, each one carving, polishing and shaping the sloping foothills, leveling the prairies, and carving basins, valleys and lake beds. Time had no known beginning or ending, but when the time was right the temperature warmed the earth and the earth bloomed. The grasses, the flowers, the bushes, and the trees grew and reproduced until the earth was covered with a green mantle nurtured by the gentle rains from the sea.

As the ice receded, it left thick glaciers circling the mountain peaks. As the icy glaciers began to melt, rivers were formed and began their descent down the mountainsides, winding through the valleys and prairies to drain into the marine waters of the inland sea below. And so it was that nature had its way in those days before man came to this land.

Trees grew on the mountain slopes, the grasses grew on the prairies, berries appeared on the hillsides and rushes emerged in the swampy marshlands. Birds came to nest in sheltered

places. The deer, the elk, the bear and their friends inhabited the forested highlands. The rabbits and squirrels found homes in the lowlands. The rivers filled with salmon, and the oysters and clams bedded in the sandy shore of the marine waters of the inland sea. It was then that all was ready. It was then that the people came.

The People Who Came –*Chapter 2*

When the first Nisqually people arrived here thousands of years ago, they came not by the Asia land bridge as many are led to believe. Instead, it is said that they traveled north from the area of the hot and arid Great Basin to find a new home. A Nisqually travel legend relates how the people once lived near the sun in the lands of Central America, where the great ice sheets could not reach them. As the ice fields receded, many Indian groups followed the melting ice into what is today known as the Great Basin. There they found food, water and material with which to build their homes. It is not known how many generations lived in the adobe houses built on the hillsides. At a certain time the earth in that region began to warm and the land became dry and barren. The mountains there became very angry and began to grumble and send out large deposits of volcanic ash. When the earth shook, the people became afraid.

Groups of Indian people once again began to move northward. It is not known how much time passed as the people slowly made their way to a cooler climate. One of the groups that traveled into what is now called eastern Washington stopped at a point where a tall mountain range lay to their left towards the setting sun. They crossed over the pass just south of the mountain peak that they in time would call by the name of Ta-co-bet, the peak called Ta-ho-ma by those who lived on its eastern flank.

This group of Indian people, who would later call themselves the Squalli-absch, made camp on Squaitz Creek, the creek that today is known by the name of Skate Creek. The people could hardly believe their good fortune. All around them lay a land of green forests filled with a bounty of wildlife, berries and roots. A mighty glacier-fed river that flowed westward down the mountainside held the promise that more lands lay below.

A Partnership With Nature
—Chapter 3

The Nisqually people were to learn a new code from this rich natural world. They became fish people. The Nisqually River and its tributaries were filled at different times of the year with six kinds of salmon. The people learned to build weirs which were placed in the slower, calmer, tributary waters. They learned how to prepare and preserve the salmon for winter use. They dug shellfish on the sandy marine beaches. Trails reached from the mountain villages to the inland sea.

They hunted the lowlands and foothills for the deer, the elk and the bear. They gathered and dried the many kinds of nuts and berries. They dug the roots and bulbs found on the prairies, in the meadows and the marshlands. Woodland birds and water-fowl were caught in nets and snares. The people learned to use fire, a kin of the sun's energy, to bake, roast and dry their food; and as spring and summer brought an abundance of nature's bounty, they learned to dry and store food for the winter use.

From the cedar trees they fashioned their house planks and canoes; and the cedar bark was used to make their clothing. From the grasses, rushes, roots and bark they made baskets and weaved mats. They gathered and dried special plants for herbal medicines. Their tools and utensils were made from stones, bones and wood.

The physical characteristics of the Nisquallies took on a new form as they developed short husky bodies with the broad shoulders needed to paddle their canoes. They walked the trails along the river and through the forests. The old ways and the new ways merged into one as they learned to survive in their new surroundings. They practiced conservation and respected the natural forces that supplied their needs. A partnership developed between man and nature.

As time passed a portion of the village people moved down the Nisqually River—first to the area near the present day town of Elbe, then to the Mashel River, a tributary of the Nisqually River. At both sites, villages were established. Later on, the people migrated downstream to where the forests ended and the prairies began. As time passed, the people multiplied in number as they intermarried with members of their neighboring tribes who had established themselves on the Puyallup and Cowlitz rivers. Many more villages appeared until they stretched down to the mouth of the Nisqually River where it emptied into the great inland sea called the Whulge, which today is called Puget Sound.

The people named the river "Squalli" after the name of the grasses that grew tall and blossomed on the prairie lands. They then called themselves the "Squalli-absch" meaning "the people of the grass country, the people of the river."

The Nisqually River watershed and the neighboring streams supplied food, shelter and clothing. This is how it all happened; this is as it has been told.

12

When asked of the Nisqually elders how long the Nisqually people had lived on the Nisqually River, the answer was "We have always been here. There were no other people here when we came. If others had been here before us, they left no signs. The earth alone holds that knowledge."

Today the Squalli-absch are known as the Nisqually. Through time, "absch," meaning "the people of," was dropped and the prefix "Nis" was added, so that today the descendants of the first people are known by the anglicized name of Nisqually. The name of the river has undergone a similar name change. The prairie grass alone has retained the name of squalli.

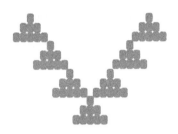

Mountain: Small triangles are placed inside wide zigzag bands that are either stepped or straight-sided. This design is quite common throughout the Puget Salish and has several variations. Observed among Duwamish, Steilacoom, Sauk-Suiattle and Suquamish.

From: Crow's Shells: Artistic Basketry of Puget Sound by Nile Thompson and Carolyn Marr

PART TWO: Relationship to the Mountain

Mashel Falls ca. 1905. Photo by A.H. Barnes, University of Washington Libraries, Special Collections, 188A

The Spirituality of the Nisqually – *Chapter 4*

To understand the relationship the Nisquallies developed with the mountain they called Ta-co-bet, one must first understand some facets of their underlying spiritual beliefs. Discussing only portions of the traditional Nisqually religion here should not in any way minimize the importance of the entire spectrum of their beliefs. Living in the natural world, without the complexities of today, they developed a coexistence with nature which included respect and appreciation of its beneficent forces as well as fear of its demonic forces.

The religion of an Indian person could not be separated from the rest of his life, for it permeated his every thought and action. He believed that the Great Mystery, the Sagale Tyee, the highest of spirit powers, did not breathe his spirit into man alone, but that all of earth's creatures possessed a spirit of some degree. Not only the animals were thus endowed, but each manifestation of nature was represented by a different spirit. Thus there existed a spirit of the wind, storm, thunder, lake, forest, swamp, light, dark, and so on. The Nisqually bestowed names onto those spirits which surrounded him and, at the time of puberty, most accepted one of these spirits as his own guardian spirit and partner in life.

Not all of the spiritual manifestations were friendly. Some were good or benevolent forces, others were evil or demon-like. To make things more complicated, some spirit forces had two faces.

For example, the spirit of the wind could blow gentle breezes but, if angered, could blow over trees and destroy homes.

For the Nisqually, Doquebulth represented the spirit of light or the good forces. Seatco represented the demon of the dark or evil forces.

Indian people showed their appreciation to the benevolent spirit forces through songs, dances and prayers. They attempted to avoid the evil forces, which they feared. If this was not possible, they tried to appease them or at least to not provoke them to anger.

When considering the relationship the Nisqually people formed with the mountain which they called Ta-co-bet, one must include the good and evil spiritual aspects of their religious beliefs, for the mountain area housed both forces. In the Nisqually way of thinking both kinds of spirit forces demanded their respect. For the good spirits there evolved a sense of appreciation for all of the benefits from the mountain. For the evil spirits there was established a feeling of fear and a desire to avoid them at all costs.

Appreciation of the Mountain Forces – *Chapter 5*

The traditional Nisqually people stood in awe of the importance of the mountain in their everyday life. They called the mountain Ta-co-bet, their name for "nourishing breasts." They reasoned that it was from the slopes of these snow-covered peaks that the icy glacier began its descent downhill to furnish the waters for the Nisqually River. It was the place where the waters began. The river was the lifeblood of the people. Not only did the river connect all of the many villages into one tribe, but it was the home of the salmon, the Nisquallies' main source of food.

Many times throughout his lifetime, a traditional Nisqually would be reminded of the travel legend and the previous home of his people, the place where the sun dried and baked the earth. But here it was different. In this land the water spirit dominated. What moisture didn't fall from the sky as rain came down the mountainside in the wide and raging Nisqually River. Numerous earth springs and lakes spawned the smaller streams, tributaries of the mother river.

The labor and fruit of the water world was everywhere. A mantle of green vegetation—trees, bushes, ferns, vines, flowers, grasses—covered the mountain slopes, crept over the lowlands, through the meadows and onto the prairies. Bulbs and roots were nourished beneath the earth's sod; berries developed on the bushes and vines; and it all grew and ripened in the summer sun.

Where an abundance of vegetation existed there appeared an abundance of wildlife. The birds and waterfowl made their homes in the woodlands and marshes. Fish filled the streams. Shellfish came to dwell on the saltwater beaches. The people were never without food.

Although perhaps not as scientific as today's meteorologists, the Nisqually Indian people had early detected that the rain-laden clouds coming from the great body of water known today as the Pacific Ocean were hindered from passing from sight into the eastern sky by the high silhouette of the Cascade Mountains. The rain clouds would bump against the mountain range and drop their moisture on its western slopes.

The Nisquallies had no assurance the Great Creator would not dry up this land as he had thousands of years before in the lands from which they came. But here, they sensed a lasting bond between the ocean and the mountains. Just as the appearance of the rainbow signified to the children of Noah that there would never be another flood, here the Great One had planted a row of high mountains on the eastern skyline as a reminder to the people of the Nisqually country that as long as the two remained in partnership there would always be water.

Nevertheless, this amazing phenomenon was never completely taken for granted by the Nisquallies. Daily prayers of thanksgiving were uttered for their "daily bread" and for the water that made it possible.

Fear and Respect of the Mountain Forces – *Chapter 6*

Reaction to the mysteries of the things not known by the traditional Nisqually people took on the forms of fear and respect. Both were profound responses given to a strong and powerful spirit entity, be it good or bad, or both.

The beneficent forces of the mountain seemed to indicate that the creator of this immense landform had set the natural forces in motion. He left in charge a collection of powerful spirit forces who fiercely guarded their domain. They decreed their home as sacred ground and declared that no human should set foot above the line they had drawn, above which even vegetation did not dare to grow.

The guardian spirits left in charge were familiar to the Nisqually who called each one by name. They knew which ones could be gentle and kind as well as which ones could be strong and destructive if angered. There was Laliad, the spirit of the wind, whose gentle breezes could move the rain clouds about in the sky or rustle the leaves of the trees to make music. Laliad could also display a more destructive side and had the power to overturn huge trees in its fury. It was known that Laliad was the forerunner of Wha-quoddie, the spirit of the storm, so when the wind began to behave harshly, the people braced themselves for a possible storm.

Wha-quoddie, the storm king, was perceived as a monstrous thunderbird who controlled the rain clouds and whose whim could create a storm. It was believed he produced the sound of thunder by flapping his wings and made lightning by flashing his eyes. The story goes that Wha-quoddie often traveled to the ocean for food. While there, he would, if he wished, gather up all the dark storm clouds and return with them to his home on the mountain. He would move his wings and flash his eyes as the storm moved across the lands of the Nisqually. The Indian people were frightened by Wha-quoddie's angry display, but accepted that he also was the one who brought the rain that sustained their land.

There were other dangers on the mountain slopes that were not as predictable as the wind and the storms. Those forces appeared with little warning. Volcanic action from within the heart of the mountain would be known only when the earth began to shake and rumble. Although this action had not yet taken place on the slopes of Ta-co-bet, the chance of volcanic eruption remained a constant fear. Whenever smoke or steam was seen rising from the mountain top, the people thought of it as a possible sign of worse things to come. The tribal elders would point to the smoke and remind their children and grandchildren of the mountains in the southlands from which their ancestors had come, mountains that hurled out hot lava. That lava lay within the heart of this mountain seemed evident from the steam clouds on the mountain's top. If the spirits of the mountain became very angry, it was feared ashes and rocks would shoot high into the sky and bring destruction to the lands of the Nisqually. It had happened to the lands of the Cowlitz; it could happen here.

Avalanches of snow and rocks could be set off by unseen forces, like the sun melting the heavy snowpack or fierce winds roaring

around the high mountain slopes. Steep crags and deep crevasses camouflaged by new fallen snow were placed strategically over the face of the higher slopes as a deterrent against those who would enter. These places were just as deadly as land mines in a battleground, but these were designed by nature. Even the agile mountain goat needed to know when and when not to tempt nature in the high places.

The turbulent winter blizzards and fierce winds were watched by the people in the lands below. While there were many days when the moving cloud cover hid the mountain from view, the Indian people looked toward the mountain for signs of approaching weather.

There was no doubt that the natural forces protected the mountain slopes where the air was less and breathing more difficult. The advantage the Nisqually Indian people had over the non-Indians who would come later and attempt to scale the mountain was the knowledge of the two faces of mother nature. When angered, nature protected her own.

Respect for Ta-co-bet came not only out of fear of the natural forces of nature, but also from appreciation of the beauty and solemnity the mountain bestowed upon the countryside. Its lofty snowcapped peak standing against the blue sky of the day and looming in the dark sky of evening was a constant and beautiful part of their lives. The mountain was always there, never failing, friend, companion, home of the most high of spirit powers even when sequestered behind the clouds. If the Sagale Tyee, the Creator, the Great One, the mightiest of all spirit powers had a home, it surely must be on the peak of Ta-co-bet.

Butterfly: Triangles are arranged in vertical rows with points down, usually touching each other. Baskets from the Skagit, Snohomish, Suquamish, Nisqually, Duwamish, Sauk-Suiattle and Twana have been observed with this design.

From: Crow's Shells: Artistic Basketry of Puget Sound by Nile Thompson and Carolyn Marr

PART THREE: Legends

Nisqually River canyon, southwest of Paradise. Photo by A.H. Barnes. University of Washington Libraries, Special Collections, BARNES211

What Are Legends? – *Chapter 7*

Indian history is oral history, carried down through the ages by stories that were told and retold until they were memorized. Legends of the traditional Nisqually people could be divided into several categories, but only three types of legends will be considered here.

The first group contain "the historical legends." Although sometimes expanded by the one telling the story, they are believed to be basically true. The second group deals with "the how and why legends," which attempt to explain a natural activity such as how the night turns into day, how the jaybird got the notch on the top of his head and why the deer has such thin legs. These legends always seem to make good sense and often, compared to today's analysis, come very close to scientifically accepted explanations. The third kind of legends are sometimes called "the fantasy stories" in which animals take on human aspects such as the Changer and other mythical characters who could work magic on those under their spell.

Although the stories could be told and retold by anyone in the tribe who had a firsthand experience worthy of repeating, the task of storytelling was usually left up to the grandparents, the elders of the tribe. Grandparents seemed to have more time to spend with the children. They would help the busy mother and keep the small ones interested by telling stories about "the good old days." During the day the children would gather around the older one and plead for a story. And so, the old and the young would sit on a log, a grassy knoll, or the riverbank and hold their school. At dusk they would gather around the inside fireplace and the children would ask for stories they had heard many times over. Soon they themselves could tell the story from their memory.

One way to keep the children in camp was to remind them of the story of Seatco, the crazy man who roamed the woods looking for little children to steal and carry away to his den deep in the forest.

The story was similar to today's bogeyman tales. Seldom did a child wander too far from the village for fear of being picked up and transported away to the old man's house and, perhaps, becoming his next meal.

Probably the most favored stories in the "how and why" department dealt with the spirit forces who were good, bad, or both. Not only were these stories entertaining, but each one taught a valuable lesson. How better to warn the children to stay away from Whe-atchee Lake than by telling them the story of the demon that lived beneath the water. The demon, it was said, would occasionally stick its black hand up out of the water to remind would-be molesters to stay away.

How mountains were formed and fought with each other were only a few of the geographical or landform stories told by the Nisqually and other Indian tribes of the lower Puget Sound area.

Legends of the Mountain – *Chapter 8*

These legends concern various mountain topics and have been compiled from a variety of sources. The legends are told here as originally published to retain the feeling and flow of the old narrative style.

How Puget Sound and the Cascade Mountain Range Originated

"In the beginning when the land was new, the waters came only from the ground. At a certain time these ground waters in the inland area dried up and the plants began to die. The inland people sent a messenger to Ocean and asked him to send moisture to them. He responded by sending his children Cloud and Rain to the dry country. Soon the streams were full and the plants grew again. When Ocean asked for the return of his children, the inland people refused to send them home for fear their land would dry up as soon as they left. They became greedy and dug pits and filled them with water. Ocean promised that their land would not dry up, but still the inland people refused to return his children. In desperation, Ocean appealed to the Great Spirit to punish the inland people.

"The Great Spirit responded. He leaned down from the sky and, scooping up earth, made the Cascade Mountains as a wall between Ocean and the dry country and doomed the latter to always be dry. The long deep hole from where he had scooped the dirt soon filled with water and later became known as Puget Sound. Still today the Cascade Mountains stand as a barrier between the ocean and the dry country, a reminder to the inland people of their greed. The pits, one of which is Lake Chelan, remain full of water. Ocean has not forgotten. He gives them but very little moisture as he continues to grieve for his children." (Adapted from "The Origin of Puget Sound and the Cascade Range" by Ella Clark in *Indian Legends of the Pacific Northwest* (Carpenter: 1977, 2-3)

How Ohanapecosh Got Its Name

"Ohanapecosh was the name given to the river and springs in the extreme upper end of Lewis County, 12 miles above Packwood.

"An old Indian up there gives the following meaning of the word: A long time ago a big Indian went to the high rock bank just above the large blue hole of clear water near the hot springs. He was dressed up in his best, having many colors on his costume. When he looked over the bank down into the hole he saw his reflection in that sparkling water and the only thing he said was 'Ohanapecosh!' which means to the white man 'looking down on something wonderful.'

"The question was asked of this old Indian if it meant that the pool was wonderful. His reply was 'No, this Indian saw wonderful Indian there.'" (Newspaper article, unknown origin, circa 1935)

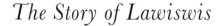

The Story of Lawiswis

"One of the most beautiful of the Indian myths connected with Paradise is that of Lawiswis, the rose bride of Nekahni, the great spirit of the upper air. According to this legend, Nekahni in addition to his general superintendence to the world and all that it contained, kept bands of wild goats about the cliffs which we call Gibraltar. Lawiswis was a beautiful nymph having the nature of a seashell and also of a rose. Nekahni made for her a bower of pure white roses down below Paradise, somewhere on the open slopes above the raging torrents of the Paradise River. There he would visit her at times and then, leaving her in care of the roses, which were supposed to be endowed with some kind of life not very distinctly understood, he would ascend through the flowery meadows of Paradise to the glaciers where the wild goats loved to sport.

"Now the Indians believed as firmly as we do in good spirits and bad, and as a standoff for the sweet and innocent Lawiswis their imagination constructed a hideous 'skookum' called Memalek. Memalek was the incarnation of everything that was vile and cruel and wicked. Her fingers were of cougar claws and her wolf robe was fastened together with the tails of snakes. By reason of the very virtue and beauty of Lawiswis, Memalek hated her correspondingly. Accordingly, one day when Nekahni was high up on the pinnacle of Gibraltar, Memalek, with a retinue of poison snakes with hideous vipers of every description, went to the rose bower of the fairy queen. Lawiswis lay sleeping in her innocent beauty unconscious of evil. The guardian roses, as pure and white as she and having then not a single thorn, were awake and on guard as soon as they saw the approach of the hideous skookum and her attendant monsters. Just as these were about to force their way into the bower to strike and poison to death Nekahni's bride, a miracle occurred. Nekahni was far away; what could be done? Though personally out of reach, he felt the signal through the air of danger to his loved one and with a creative force which overleaped the barriers of space he inspired the roses to be transformed at once from innocent white to fighting red and to bring out all over their extending sharp thorns. Appalled by the fiery red before them and stung by the barbed spines, the shaky cohorts fell back upon the edge of the consecrated bower and slunk away with their disappointed leader, Memalek, to their dens in the depths of the Nisqually Canyon. And so Lawiswis was saved, and thus there were red roses in the world as well as white, and the roses henceforth had thorns." (Lymon: 1906, 450)

Wha-Quoddie, The Thunder Bird

"About a mile east of Buckley, in the valley of the White River, stands a small mountain peak. It is about a thousand feet high and is surrounded by the level prairie. Its southern base comes down to the river, yet far enough away to permit the ancient Yakima trail to go by on its way down from the Naches Pass. Here the glacier waters break from the mountain canyons; the green prairies so loved by

the Squally-absch dot the forests from this point to Puget
Sound. This almost perpendicular peak is 'Enim-tla'
or Thunder-mountain, and is the resting place of Wha-
quoddie, the thunder-bird. Wha-quoddie is a monster
bird; he advances in and above the storm cloud; thunder
is produced by the flapping of his wings, and lightning
by the flash of his eyes. He is the spirit of the storm; he
creates clouds and controls the rains. He goes out to the
ocean for food which accounts for the meteorological fact
that the rain clouds and thunder storms come from the
Pacific. When the thunder rolls and rumbles from the dark
advancing cloud, filling the valley and the canyons above
Enim-tla with distant reverberations, when the dark storm
advances and the lightning flashes, it is noticed that Wha-
quoddie has returned to his mountain home from another
trip to the ocean. The Squally-absch compare their rich
lands, flowing rivers, waving forests, their fisheries and
berry lands with the sandy plains of the Yakimas, and give
the praise to Wha-quoddie, who brings the rains; at the
same time they fear the noise of the thunder and the stroke
of lightning." (Wickersham: 1898, 349)

Chan-a-hoh

The Chan-a-hoh is a great bird that lives by the lake on the
south fork of the Cowlitz River near Mount St. Helens. It
feeds upon men and cannot be killed with arrows or bullets.
It is known to the Nisquallies by the name of Chan-a-hoh.
The Chan-a-hoh is a different bird than the thunderbird.
(Rewritten from Gibbs: 1856, 14)

Why There Are No Snakes on Mount Rainier

"There is an Indian legend that does away entirely with the supposition that there were any vipers or poisonous reptiles anywhere about the mountain. And in fact in so far as we have been able to learn there is none such there at the present time. This legend is a sort of Indian version of the Noachian deluge. According to this, Sahalie (which is just another name for Nekahni or the great spirit) was so displeased with the general badness, both of the Indians and of the animals round about Mount Tahoma, that he determined to make away with them entirely. Accordingly he told a certain 'tomanowas' man to take his bow and shoot his arrow into the cloud which hung over the mountain. Following out the direction the man was astonished to see the arrow stick into the cloud. But, following the voice of Sahalie, he shot another which pierced the first, and so on until he had a long line of arrows extending all the way from the cloud to the earth. Still carrying out the directions given him by Sahalie, the man caused his wife and children and then certain good animals to crawl up the arrow line until they reached the cloud. Going up last of all himself, he found, just as he was entering into the cloud, that a whole procession of snakes and every kind of evil creature were swarming up the line behind him. Therefore he hastily tore the arrows apart and the whole swarm was precipitated down upon the mountainside. Immediately after there came an enormous deluge, which covered the entire country up to the line of snow upon the mountain. As a result of this deluge all the snakes and

34

other evil beasts were drowned, and when the waters subsided and when the 'tomanowas' man with his family and the good animals had descended, they found a new world in which there were no snakes." (Lymon: 1906, 451)

The Miser of Mount Rainier

There are several versions of the legend about the miser who traveled to the top of the mountain and in his greed was condemned to sleep away many years of his life. It was first printed in the book *Canoe and Saddle* written by Theodore Winthrop as told to him by a Nisqually named Hamitchou in 1853. The miser was the grandfather of Hamitchou. The following version is a condensed form of the legend:

"There was an old man living near the Mountain who was very avaricious and desirous of obtaining much 'hiaqua'— which is shell money still common among the Indians of the Sound. This old Indian was on very intimate terms with Sahale and kept begging him to supply him with more money by magic, for the long and laborious processes of saving and hoarding were too slow for the old Indian. Sahale, however, was aware that this greed for hiaqua was liable to make the old man a victim of Kahahete, the chief of the demons, and therefore he always refused to grant him any magic power.

"But Moosmoos, the Elk divinity, obtained a tamanowas [spirit] power over the old Indian and whispered magic in his ear, telling him that on the summit of the Mountain he might find much hiaqua and become the richest man in the world. Going back to his camp, he informed his wife that he was going on a long hunt —but in reality he was setting forth for the summit of the Mountain. The first day he climbed almost to the top, and next morning at the rising of the sun he stood upon the crest. He discovered that there was a great valley on the summit, filled except in one place with snow. Here was a lake of black water, and at one end of it there were three black rocks. The old man was confident that those were the tamanowas rocks; for one was shaped like a salmon's head, another like a camas root, and the third like the head of his own totem or divinity, Moosmoos, the elk.

"The old Indian, observing these symbolic rocks concluded that this must be the place where the hiaqua was secreted. He began to dig at once with the elk horn pick which he had brought for the purpose, at the feet at the elk shaped rock. At this gesture, a number of otter came out of the lake and gathered around in a circle. When the man had struck the ground a number of times equal to the number of otter, they began to pound the ground with their tails. Still he continued to dig, and about sundown he overturned a large rock under which he discovered a large cavity completely filled with hiaqua—great strings of it, and enough to make him the richest of all men.

"But now the greedy adventurer made a great mistake. He loaded himself with the strings of hiaqua and left not a single shell as an offering to the tamanowas powers by whose magic he had made the discovery. Sahale was greatly displeased at such ungrateful conduct, and all the tamanowas

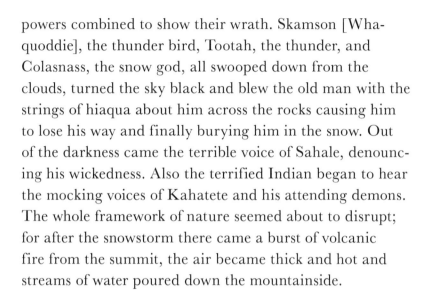

powers combined to show their wrath. Skamson [Wha-quoddie], the thunder bird, Tootah, the thunder, and Colasnass, the snow god, all swooped down from the clouds, turned the sky black and blew the old man with the strings of hiaqua about him across the rocks causing him to lose his way and finally burying him in the snow. Out of the darkness came the terrible voice of Sahale, denouncing his wickedness. Also the terrified Indian began to hear the mocking voices of Kahatete and his attending demons. The whole framework of nature seemed about to disrupt; for after the snowstorm there came a burst of volcanic fire from the summit, the air became thick and hot and streams of water poured down the mountainside.

"In spite of all of this confusion of nature, the Indian retained his consciousness, and he began to think of how he might propitiate the offended deities. He dropped one of the strings of hiaqua as an offering—but this seems to have been a mere mockery, and the demons kept howling at him in derisive tones, 'Hiaqua! Haiqua!' Then the Indian flung away one string after another until they were all gone, and fell upon the ground exhausted and entered into a deep sleep. When he awoke he found that he was at the same place where he had fallen asleep on the night before he set out for the summit.

"Being very hungry he set about gathering camas roots with which to refresh himself, and while eating he began to have many thoughts in regard to his life and doings. His 'tum-tum' (heart) was much softened as he contemplated his greed for hiaqua. He found that he no longer cared for it, and that his mind was calm, tranquil and benevolent. Moreover, when he looked at himself in a pool he discovered that he had changed marvelously. His hair had become long and white as snow. The Mountain itself had changed its form. The sun shone brightly, the trees glistened with new leaves and the mountain meadows were sweet with the perfume of many flowers. Birds sang in the trees, and the great mountain towered calm, tranquil and majestic into the deep blue sky, glistening with the fallen snow. All nature seemed to rejoice and the old Indian found that he was almost in a new world.

"Then he seemed to remember where he was, and he made his way without difficulty to his camp. There he found an old woman with white hair whom he did not recognize at first, but soon he discovered her to be his own 'klootchman.' She told him that he had been gone many suns and moons, and that in the meantime she had been digging camas and trading for hiaqua, of which she had accumulated much. The old Indian now perceived all the mistakes of his former avaricious life and settled down on the banks of the Nisqually in peace and contentment. He became a great tamanowas man and a counselor and advisor to the Indians in all kinds of trouble. He was worshipped by them for his wisdom and experience and benevolence, as well as for his strange experience upon the summit of the Mountain." (U.S. Department of the Interior mountain information papers)

Mountain Lake Myths

The Nisqually Indian people were very superstitious about lakes, swamps and places where water tended to gather but not disperse or move. They believed a race of demons inhabited the lakes called the Jug-wa or Zug-wa. Nisqually Lake, Spanaway Lake, and Steilacoom Lake were believed to be the abode of such demons.

There were many small lakes and pools on the mountain in very quiet and lonely places. Many Indian people believed that these isolated places were the home of spirits long since departed and that these spirits did not wish to be disturbed. Therefore they went to all lengths not to offend them by even rippling the water. They did not get their drinking or cooking water from these lakes nor did they water their horses from them for fear of offending these spirits. They did not even throw a rock into the water of a lake.

There are those Indian people who believed that if the water from a lake was disturbed that it would rain. One young man had gone with his family to the mountains to pick huckleberries. He decided to test the validity of the lake spirits. Being warm and tired of hunting berries, he sneaked over to a lake, undressed and went for a swim. As he got out of the water, clouds gathered and it began to rain. The rain came down in torrents. That evening in camp, it was asked if anyone had troubled the lake. The young man admitted he had gone for a swim that day. He was admonished not to do so again. The following day, deciding again to test the theory, the young man dislodged and rolled a large stone down the hillside, its momentum sending it plunging into the lake. Although it was a sunny day, within a short time the sky was overcast with dark clouds and the rain came down in torrents, surpassing the rainstorm of the previous day. The group gathered in camp, talked over their feelings of superstitious "awe" and decided to break camp and leave, feeling that if they remained longer some dire calamity might overtake them. (Rewritten from Bagley: 1930, 42)

Glaciers of the southwest slope as viewed from a portion of Indian Henry's Park. Nisqually name for this place is No-ach-a-muich. Photo by A.H. Barnes, 1907. University of Washington Libraries Special Collections, BARNES386 .

Other Nisqually Legends – *Chapter 9*

T he legends extend beyond the mountain to encompass
all aspects of nature. We now turn our attention to some
of these other topics–the swamps and forests, light and wind,
snakes and birds. As with the mountain legends, they are told
here as originally published to retain the feeling and flow of the
old narrative style.

Tu-ba-dy, the Spirit of the Swamps and Thickets

"Tu-ba-dy is the spirit of the swamps and thickets. When
the Squally-absch hear the voice of Tu-ba-dy they become
lost and wander aimlessly about. Tu-ba-dy does no damage
to the person, no one can see it, but simply to hear its voice
causes one to become lost, prevents one from knowing the
right direction or finding one's home. In all cases where
persons are lost in the woods, it is because they have heard
the cry of Tu-ba-dy who turned them in the wrong direction." (Wickersham: 1898, 350)

Zach-ad, the Spirit of the Swamps

"Zach-ad is another spirit of the swamps. It is heard to cry at
night in the swamps, in dense woods or other lonely places,
but particularly out near Spanaway Lake. It is derived from
the Squally word 'to cry' when one's relative or friend dies,
and the voice of this spirit is an omen of death. Not that it
will cause the death, for it merely announces a fact known
to it through its intimacy with the spirits of the dead from
Otlas-skio (home of the dead)." (Wickersham: 1898, 350)

Doquebulth, the Spirit of the Light

"Doquebulth, the Changer, represents the highest form of good in the polytheism of the Squally-absch, while the fear of Seatco, the demon of the dark forest, was the most pronounced feature of their demonology. Doquebulth was a culture hero; he changed men into animals and fish and transformed his wives into the sleek brown-coated elk; he taught the Indians how to make and use the bow and arrow; he created the salmon and other food fish and taught the Squally-absch to make traps. The story of his birth in the stars and descent to earth is an unfailing source of interest to Indian auditors." (Wickersham: 1898, 346-7)

Seatco, the Demon of the Dark Forests

"Doquebulth, the spirit of light, finds his opposite in Seatco, the evil one, the demon of the dark forests. Seatco is a malicious demon having the form of an Indian, but larger, quick and stealthy. He inhabits the dark recesses of the woods, where his campfires are often seen; he sleeps by day but sallies forth at dusk for 'a night of it.' He robs traps, breaks canoes, steals food and other portable property; he waylays the belated traveler, and is said to have killed all those whose bodies are found dead. To his malicious cunning is credited all the unfortunate and malicious acts which cannot be otherwise explained. He steals children and brings them up as slaves in his dark retreats; he is a constant menace to the disobedient child, and is the object of fear and terror to all." (Wickersham: 1898, 348)

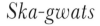

Ska-gwats

"Ska-gwats, a shaman, was jealous of the power and reputation of Doquebulth, and sought to kill him. As he sat singing his hatred to Doquebulth, the Changer came by. Ska-gwats did not recognize him. Doquebulth said, 'What are you singing about? Sing it again.' The answer was, 'I am making needles with which to kill Doquebulth.' The Changer asked for the needles, and having received them, suddenly seized Ska-gwats and thrust them into his legs and arms, struck him a blow, changed him into a deer saying, 'You were not made for a warrior, but to be eaten as food.' And Ska-gwats, the deer, has the bone needles in his ankles to this day." (Wickersham: 1898, 349-50)

Whe-atchee

"Whe-atchee is the Indian name of Steilacoom Lake. It is given to that body of water because a female demon of that name lives in its depths. No Indian ever bathes in that lake for fear of Whe-atchee. When she shows herself, it is by raising her head and right arm out of the water, elevating the little finger and the thumb and closing the middle fingers, and saying 'Here is my Whe-atchee.' On account of the fear of this demon, this lake is shunned by the Squally-absch as an evil place." (Wickersham: 1898, 350)

La-liad, the Spirit of the Wind

"La-liad is the spirit of the wind. When the Indian children hear the sharp musical sound of the wind at night as it cuts the corner of their lowly home, it is accepted as the call of La-liad. When the trees bend musically before the breeze, when a stronger wind overturns the great fir and cedar trunks, it is the force of La-liad, the spirit of the wind. He is the attendant of Wha-guoddie, the storm king and usually precedes his coming. Every sound of the wind, every whistle, moan or sigh, even the roar of the storm, is the voice of La-liad." (Wickersham: 1898, 350)

Swo-cock

"'The man in the moon,' according to Squally tradition, is a female. Swo-cock was a female frog who stole Doquebulth's magic bag. For which theft she was condemned by him to stand forever in the moon, in sight of all the Squally-absch, holding the stolen bag in her hand–a solemn public warning against theft." (Wickersham: 1898, 350)

How Ski-ki the Blue Jay Got His Topknot

"Soon after he returned to earth, the child of the stars was stolen by Pup-pe-de and carried to the land of Sunset–behind a great portal that regularly rose and fell. Their efforts to recover him make a long chapter in the sagas of Fish land. The deer, bear, crow, eagle and many others,

were sent for him, but all were crushed at the danger-
ous portal. At last Ski-ki, the jay bird, was sent. He sat
just outside the portal until it began to rise, when he went
through in a flash–not quite enough, however, for the closing walls crushed the top of his head and Ski-ki yet turns
his head sideways to the Squally-absch so that his topknot
may remind them of the debt of gratitude they owe him."
(Wickersham: 1898, 348)

The Birth of Doquebulth

"Two comely sisters of the tribe of Squally-absch had re-
tired to sleep beneath the shelter of a mat home. Above
their heads the mats parted somewhat, and through the
rent they gazed upon the starry heaven. Like many another pair of maidens they began to talk of marriage.
The Indians imagine that men are frequently placed in
the sky by some supernatural power, and there shine as
stars. Referring to these curious legends, one of the sisters
inquired of the other which of the stars above them she
would chose for a husband. The answer was, 'the bright
one.' The other chose the red star and dreaming of marriage with these far away star men they fell asleep. When
they awoke they found that they had been transported to
the stars. They met the bright and red star men of their
fancy and became their wives; and so happy and peace-
ful was their honeymoon that they forgot in some degree
the loss of home and friends on the far off earth. To the
eldest of the sisters, by this astral marriage, was born
Doquebulth, a beautiful child, and one possessed with the

power to change the very character of matter. He could change a man or a woman into a rock, an elk or a bird; he could upturn mountains, break the surface of the earth into lakes and rivers, and could change the whole aspect of the earth.

"As with other Indian wives, it was the duty of these two sisters to seek food for their husbands. Each day they wandered out to dig fern roots (tuddy) to mix with salmon eggs and to make 'tsad-ack.' They were cautioned by their husbands, 'Do not dig deep, take only the fern roots nearest the surface.'

"This injunction they followed for a long time, but Eve-like, one day one of them said, 'Why do our husbands require us to take that part of the tuddy nearest the surface, why not dig deeper?

"No sooner suggested than they began to dig. Deeper and deeper they dug, until the very bottom root of tuddy was reached, when, upon another stroke of the elk-horn, they pierced the surface of Star-land. Peering, with astonishment, through this hole, they saw far below them the waving forests and blue waters, the clouds and mountains of earth, their old home. 'Ah,' they said, 'there is our country; there is where we came from; there are our friends and parents.'

"They now began to long to go back to their own people; thereafter only the youngest dug fern roots, while the eldest began secretly to make a rope of hazel witches. After great labor the rope was completed. One day they went out as usual to dig tuddy, the mother carrying Doquebulth on her back. Having arrived at the place where their rope lay concealed, they dug a hole through Star-land, and having tied one end of their withe rope to a tree, dropped the other end through the hole and found to their great joy that it reached the earth. The youngest sister descended first, carrying Doquebulth. After she had safely reached the earth, the mother came down, and carrying the child of the stars in their arms, they traveled a little way and found their old home, where they were received with great joy. And this is the story of the birth and descent upon earth of Doquebulth, the Changer." (Wickersham: 1898, 348)

The Land of the Dead of the Nisqually

"The Squally-absch believed the world to be flat, and beneath its surface is the home of the dead, 'Otlas-skio.' Constant communication was maintained between this and the underground world by the spirits of the dead, as well as by the shamans or 'medicine men.' The country of Otlas-skio is filled with waving forests, grassy plains and running streams. Villages after the ancient type occupy the most beautiful places; the woods are filled with game and singing birds; brilliant flowers enliven the landscape and perfume the balmy air; the streams are filled with salmon and it is indeed a happy hunting ground where the dead find all their friends and relatives. Here the soul of the dead passes an eternity in pursuit of the pleasures so dear on earth; the family is again formed; the wives and children gather around the hearth fire, and the happiest period of the life on earth is resumed, never to be broken again by the pangs of separation and death.

"When the soul goes to Otlas-skio it enters the earth and goes downward; before reaching the abode of the dead it must cross a river, and a small object of value is often placed in the mouth to pay the ferryman, who awaits on the banks with a ghostly canoe to ferry the soul across. Sometimes the ferryman is absent, whereupon the soul returns to earth, re-enters the body and the person resumes life. It is thus that they explain a case of suspended animation.

"The Squally neither expected favor or reward, nor feared punishment after death. During life, however, he worshipped the beneficent forces of nature and appealed to them for aid and assistance; he feared the evil forces represented by a multitude of demons, whom he attempted to propitiate that he might escape their attacks. His ceremonial appeals to the good forces, and his attempt to allay the evil one, constituted the ritual of Nisqually theology." (Wickersham: 1898, 346)

Why the Rattlesnake Will Not Bite a Nisqually

"There are no rattlesnakes on the west side of the Cascade Mountains. Wah-push, of the tribe of the Squally-absch, went over into the Yakima country to visit his friends. While there, for some misdemeanor, he was turned into a rattlesnake by Doquebulth, and became the ancestor of the whole tribe of rattlers. His descendants have been fully informed of their ancestry and relation to the Squally-absch, and when a rattlesnake hears the Squally language spoken and thus recognizes a relative, his anger instantly subsides and he crawls from the sight of his kinsman as fast as his wriggling gait will allow. The Squally-absch assert that the rattlesnake will not bite one of their tribe." (Wickersham: 1898, 350)

The Deluge

"The Squally-absch believed as firmly as Christian people that a deluge once destroyed the nations of the world. Long ago there came a great flood, and as the waters rose higher than the hills and mountains, the Indians tied their canoes by long ropes to trees on the highest hill in their vicinity. Three points were thus used: Suc-cla-de-tsote, one of the Olympic Mountains, Ba-be-date, one of the high hills near Port Orchard, De-sha-ca, a high hill near the south end of Puget Sound. They clung to these mountains while the water rose around them, many were drowned. A few canoes, however, broke away and landed after the flood, in distant parts of the country, which explains the fact that the other tribes speak a similar language. From the few who escaped the present tribes have descended." (Wickersham: 1898, 348-9)

Swo-Quod, the Loon

"The Indian mother necessarily sought to impress the lesson of obedience to parental authority upon her child, and the story of Swo-quod, the loon, was repeated with that view. Swo-quod was a headstrong youth who frequently disobeyed his mother's instructions. He was an expert swimmer and passed much of his time in the waters and around their banks. His mother cautioned him about going to swim in Mason Lake, north of Shelton. This caution seemed only to stimulate his desire to swim in the forbidden waters; and one day he broke away from his resolution to be an obedient boy, and went into the water of the haunted lake. Instead of demons he only saw the speckled trout, 'squs-pl,' darting from side to side in the clear lake waters. In his joy he dove, and swam and finally caught a trout with his hand and swam ashore. Elated with his exercise and hungry from exertion, he kindled a fire, cooked the trout and ate it. The demon of the lake lay concealed in the beautiful speckled trout, and instantly Swo-quod was turned into a loon. Frantic at his misfortune, he flew at once to his mother's home, and circled above her head uttering the discordant cries of the loon, but trying in vain to explain his awful condition. The mother, not knowing it was her unhappy son who really loved her in spite of his disobedience, tried to kill the bird with her stick. To this day Swo-quad repeats his harsh notes of warning whenever a disobedient child is within sound of his voice." (Wickersham: 1898, 351)

The Sasquatch – *Chapter Ten*

Perhaps the biggest mystery in the annals of mountain history concerns the legends surrounding the Sasquatch, or Bigfoot, as he is sometimes called. This mythical creature cannot be considered as only one of a kind, but must be thought of as one of a species of some sort of animal-like being. In the past ten years Bigfoot has been reported as having been seen in many places throughout the world. He has even been considered as a possible cousin of the Abominable Snowman of Nepal, India.

To trace the beginning of the Sasquatch, it is necessary to turn to the traditional history of the Nisqually Indian people. In the days before the white men came to the shores of Nisqually country, the Sasquatch was very real to the Indian people of the Puget Sound area. The Nisqually people called him Seatco, the demon of the dark forests. They were terrified of him. (See the legend of Seatco by Wickersham on page 42.)

Gender changes of Seatco were common, depending on whom the storyteller was intending to impress or frighten. The gender of Wickersham's Seatco was that of a male while some Nisqually stories describe Seatco as a woman. The description of the creature also changed with each storyteller. George Gibbs, writing in 1856, described Seatco in this way:

> "The Tsiatko are described as of gigantic size, their feet eighteen inches long and shaped like a bear's. They wear no clothes, but the body is covered with hair like that of a

dog, only not so thick... they are said to live in the mountains, in holes underground, and to smell badly. They come down chiefly in the fishing season, at which time the Indians are excessively afraid of them. At the report of Tsiatko, they all run to their house, fire their guns and shout. They are visible only at night, at which time they approach the houses, steal salmon, carry off young girls and smother children. Their voices are like that of an owl, and they possess the power of charming, so that those hearing them become demented, or fall down in a swoon." (Gibbs: 1856)

Several Indian people were reported as having seen the Tsiatko according to Gibbs. One Indian woman who lived at Fort Vancouver on the Columbia River told of a having been captured by a group of Tsiatkos and taken into the woods. She lived to tell the tale of her adventure. Gibbs also reported that Leschi and Swatiltoh, both Nisqually, were said to have wounded a Tsiatko and tracked him by a trail of blood. Another Indian reported having shot at and wounding a Tsiatko while the beast was carrying off a young girl. Ke-kai-simi-loot, daughter of To-wus-tan, a former chief, and a Nisqually woman, claimed she was descended from four generations of what she called "skoo-kums." And so the stories go. (Gibbs: 1856)

An informant of Gibbs believed that these human-like animals came into being shortly after the demon race, which is to mean that the Seatco creatures were one step better in the line of creation. The informant went on to say that these Seatco people possessed manlike characteristics in that some were good and

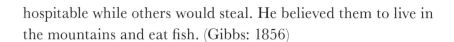

hospitable while others would steal. He believed them to live in the mountains and eat fish. (Gibbs: 1856)

The Seatco of the Indian's world slowly evolved to the white man's Sasquatch and Bigfoot. Almost every year, especially during the winter months, the footprints of Bigfoot have been reported in the snow in the mountain foothills of the Cascade Mountain Range. Attempts to take pictures of the hairy figure standing upright usually result in a blurry image of trees and shadows.

Recent sightings of Sasquatch report that he still stands upright, looks to be human-like and is covered by hair. He continues to feed on salmon and is more likely to be found on a riverbank although someone reported the beast as stealing a farmer's chickens. (Lane: 1978)

One Sasquatch hunter claims to have carried on a conversation with a colony of them in the Sierra Nevada Mountains in California. Although admitting to not knowing what the animals were saying, he coaxed them close to his campsite by repeating their call which sounded like "ooga-ga-googa." (Lane: 1979) This same person reported that the Sasquatch is difficult to track because he leaves no body wastes such as feces, which are believed to be eliminated in streams so that humans cannot find them.

In 1975, the Army Corps of Engineers included Sasquatch information in one of their publications:

"Reported to feed on vegetation and some meat, the Sasquatch is covered with long hair, except for the face and hands, and has a distinctly human-like form... is agile and strong with extremely good night vision and great shyness, leaving minimal evidence of its presence... up to 12 feet tall, weighing more than a half-ton and taking strides up to 6 feet." (T.N.T.: 1975)

Although believed to occur mainly in the western coastal mountainous regions from British Columbia to California, a group of Sasquatches was sighted on the Standing Rock Indian Reservation in South Dakota in 1977. Described as being nine feet tall, weighing 600 pounds and having a stride up to seven feet, they reportedly shrieked all night with a coyote-like scream, scaring the residents of Little Rock out of their homes to safety in the nearby town of McLaughlin. (T.N.T.: 1977)

And so, the intrigue continues. Whether real or figment of our imaginations, the Nisqually Indian legend of Seatco lives on.

The forests of Mount Rainier. Photo by A.H. Barnes, 1913. University of Washington Libraries, Special Collections, BARNES 2003

Salmon Gills: The same pattern occurs on coiled basketry throughout Puget Sound, a diagonal series of short linear segments turned outward at each end. On Twana soft twined baskets, "salmon gills" are arranged in single direction or opposing diagonals.

From: Crow's Shells: Artistic Basketry of Puget Sound by Nile Thompson and Carolyn Marr

PART FOUR: Utilization of Mountain Resources

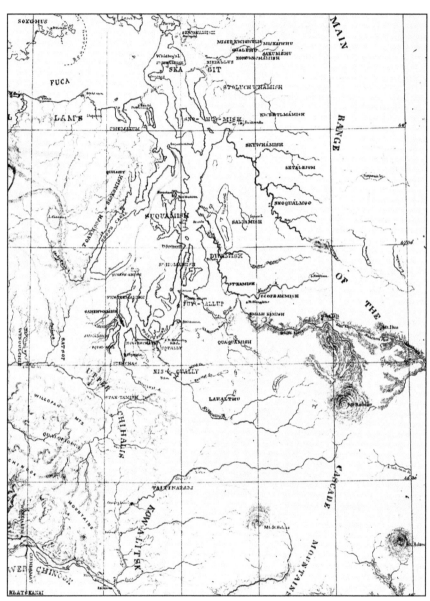

Map of the western district of Washington Territory showing the position of the Indian Tribes and the lands ceded by treaty. Drawn by George Gibbs, 1855. Washington State Historical Society.

58

The Mountain Nisqually – *Chapter 11*

The people who lived in three Indian villages on the upper portion of the Nisqually River were labeled the "Mountain Nisqually" by the British who set up a fur trading fort near the mouth of the river in 1833. The name has remained through the years. Today the Nisqually history stories still refer to the former residents of these villages as the Mountain Nisqually.

The mountain villages were never heavily populated, even in traditional times. They are considered to be the first villages of the Nisqually people who thousands of years ago had crossed the mountain pass south of Ta-co-bet. These villages suffered a constant population drain as people moved downriver.

The upper villages were occupied to the time of the Treaty of Medicine Creek of 1854 and during the war that followed. After that time all Nisqually Indian people were asked to move onto the Nisqually Indian Reservation located in the lower segment of the Nisqually River. However, some of the residents chose not to go downriver and were still residing in the mountain area when Indian Henry, a Yakima Indian, took up residence on the Mashel prairie in 1864. Others were not so fortunate. While hidden in the heavily forested area of the Mashel and Ohop waterways they met death at the hands of the Territorial Volunteers in what has been called the Mashel Massacre of 1856, a sad episode in Nisqually history.

The three mountain villages were the Squaitz or the Skate Creek village, the Lah-al-thu or the Elbe village and the

Meschal village on the Mashel River. The traditional residents of these villages were closely related to the Yakima and Klickitat Indian people who lived on the eastern slopes of the mountain. A great deal of travel and trade was carried on between the lower Nisqually villages, the upper Nisqually villages and the Yakimas. The mountain villages became a bridge between the two far ends. Intertribal marriages between the Nisquallies and the Yakimas created an atmosphere of good will and promoted an equitable social life. The Mountain Nisqually were bilingual, speaking both the Coastal Salish of the Puget Sound tribes and also the Shahaptian of their "east of the mountain" neighbors.

Squaitz Village

The Squaitz village was located on Skate Creek on Bear Prairie. In traditional times the creek was called Squaitz Creek. Elcaine Longmire described the residents of this village who continued to reside there after the Indian war.

> "The mountain tribe lived on the Skate Creek about 10 to 15 miles south of Longmire Springs. They ranged all through the mountains but wintered south of the springs. Pem-n was chief in the early days, they talked the Klickitat language ...Indian Henry married a girl of the mountain tribe, afterwards married two more so he had three." (Longmire: 1910)

Lah-al-thu Village

Little is known of the Nisqually Indian village located on the northern bank of the Nisqually River just past the present town of Elbe. Erna Gunther, noted anthropologist of the 1930s, wrote of a Nisqually village at Elbe. This was later confirmed by another anthropologist, Barbara Lane, in 1973.

Lt. A. V. Kautz, in his attempt to climb Mount Rainier in 1857, wrote of a deserted Indian camp in the vicinity and found it a convenient place to stay upon his return.

> "We passed another of our camps, and finally stopped at what evidently had been an Indian camp. The cedar bark, always to be found in such places, we anticipated would make a shelter for us in case of rain, which the clouds promised us." (Meany: 1916, 90)

In 1867, a party of surveyors seeking a pass over the mountain for the Northern Pacific Railroad indicated Indian activity in the area above Elbe and marked it on their map. (Walker: 1916, 90)

In 1870, when the Hazard Stevens party completed a successful ascent of the mountain, Stevens recalled the following in his journal.

> "We encamped on a narrow flat between the high hill just descended and the wide and noisy river, near an old ruined log-hut, the former resident of a once famed Indian medicine man, who, after the laudable custom of his race,

had expiated with his life his failure to cure a patient."
(Meany: 1916, 104)

Others have noted evidence of Indian occupation above Elbe,
but so far no real attempt has been made to pinpoint the exact
spot that George Gibbs labeled Lah-al-thu on his 1855 map.
(Gibbs: 1855)

Me-schal Village

The Me-schal village, more often referred to today as the
Mashel village, was located on the Mashel River upstream from
its junction with the Nisqually River. It is believed to have had
a larger population than the other two mountain villages. These
people were also bilingual. Me-schal was the birthplace and
home of the Nisqually chief Leschi who led the allied Indian
forces in the 1855-56 Indian War on the western side of the
Cascade Mountains. (Smith: 1940, 13)

Village Classification

There have been many conjectures by noted anthropologists concerning the classification of the three mountain villages. Many have classified them as a group separate from
the Nisqually, and names such as Mical (Spier: 1936, 42) and
Pshwanwapan (Swanton: 1952, 428) have been applied. Other
anthropologists have maintained that they were closely related
to the Taidnapam on the upper Cowlitz River to the south.

The villages' locations shown on a Nisqually Indian village
map reveal that they do stand in the upper segment of the

Nisqually River. There appear to have been no permanent villages below them from Ohop Creek to Gravelle Creek, a portion of the Nisqually River known as the middle segment, only fishing stations and camping sites. The lower segment of the river from the Gravelle Creek downriver to the Nisqually River delta apparently was most densely populated. This picture left room for the guessing game to exist among those who came later to study "Indians."

To the Nisquallies the upper river villages are Nisqually villages. One cannot ignore the years and years of history that bound together the Indian villages that stretch from one end of the Nisqually River to the other.

White-tail deer at Comet Falls, Mount Rainier National Park, Photo by Dwight
Watson, University of Washington Libraries, Special Collections, UW36715

Nature's Bounty – *Chapter 12*

From the earliest days of Nisqually history the Indian people were involved in a seasonal pursuit to gather, preserve and store their food for winter survival in their mountain foothill villages. Nature freely supplied the food items needed to meet those demands as well as the raw materials necessary to build their homes and make their clothing. The people, who for years had lived in a hot arid climate, slowly adjusted to their new surroundings. From the giant cedar trees they cut planks to build their houses and to carve out their dugout canoes, using the cedar bark to fashion their clothes. The men learned the habits of the deer, elk, and bear and very soon were able to trap and snare them. The Indian women discovered the abundance of berries and roots ready to be picked and eaten, and experimented with ways to preserve them. The discovery of the salmon, the food that would become the mainstay of their diet, rounded out the last of the basic needs necessary to survive.

Hunting

Animal paths crisscrossed through the forests and meandered overland to the river bank where the animals went to seek water. Over these runways the Indian hunter would bend a small sapling to which he attached a noose made of stout rawhide. The legs of the unsuspecting deer would become entangled in the noose and the animal would be lifted off its feet. To subdue the large and awkward bear the hunter would dig a pit on a well-worn bear trail and cover it with fir boughs, dirt and rocks.

Because the fall into the hole usually didn't kill the bear, a club was used to complete the job.

The women would roast some of the meat on sticks beside an open campfire for immediate eating. However, they cut most of the meat into thin strips and dried them on racks over a slow-burning fire, then packed the meat into storage baskets for winter use.

Small animals such as the rabbit and beaver were considered for meals only in lean times. The least preferred item was the squirrel. All three were roasted and eaten, never stored. The hunters set aerial nets between two trees to snare pheasants, grouse, geese and ducks. These birds were roasted for a quick meal.

Animal hides, even that of the small squirrel, were tanned and made into such items as bed blankets and underclothing that could be worn under the cedar-bark dresses and shirts. Bones from the dead animals made excellent tools, utensils and needles.

Fishing

The Indian breadwinners soon learned the skills of catching the salmon found in the Nisqually River and its many tributaries. They made fish traps or weirs of willow and maple sticks which were constructed across the smaller streams to block the fish as they sought to swim upstream to spawn. As the salmon milled about at the barrier, the fishermen waded into the stream and caught the fish in nets made of nettle twine.

Salmon was roasted, dried or smoked. If a fish was to be eaten immediately, the cook cleaned and cut it into chunks which she threaded onto cooking sticks to be roasted before an open fire. Salmon to be stored for winter use was cleaned, cut into strips and allowed to dry on racks over a slow-burning fire. Salmon were smoked by hanging them from the rafters inside the Indian dwelling house where the heat of the family cooking fires reached them. The dried fish was placed in large baskets and stored in a dry area. When taken from storage to be eaten during the winter months, it was soaked in water to make it more palatable. Fish was often made into pemmican by grinding it into a fine powder and mixing it with animal fat and crushed berries before molding it into little cakes. Pemmican was a favorite traveling food because of its keeping qualities.

Berries

While the men hunted deer on the lower slopes of the mountain, the women and children picked berries. The season lasted from early summer to late fall. The family traveled into the foothills and meadows to find the blueberry, salmonberry, thimbleberry, blackberry, strawberry, elderberry, salalberry, gooseberry, blackcap, and the red and blue huckleberries. Only juices could be made from the salmonberry and the blackcap as they were mushy and didn't dry well. The other berries were placed on flat racks over open fires and dried. If it rained during the drying season, cattail matting was placed over the racks to keep the berries dry. When dried, the berries were stored in large baskets. When they were to be used, they were soaked in water and ground into powder to be used for seasoning.

Roots, Bulbs, and Plants

Roots, bulbs and stems of the numerous kinds of plants that grew in the Nisqually River watershed formed an important part of the Indian diet. The women boiled or blanched tender shoots of cattails, skunk cabbage and certain other plants to further soften their fibers. They accomplished the task by placing the greens in a tightly woven cooking basket filled with water. To heat the water and cook the food, they added hot rocks from a nearby fire.

Indian women steamed bulbs such as the camas root in earthen cooking pits and stored the bulbs after they dried. They would dig the cooking pits about three or four feet deep and build a fire among the rocks in the bottom. When the fire burned out, the women wrapped the roots or bulbs in leaves and laid the bundles on the hot rocks. They added a layer of ferns, followed by about a foot of earth. They then built a fire on the top of the pit and kept it burning from several hours to several days, depending on the food being cooked. To create steam, they poured water into the pit through a hole, then plugged it with a long stick. Cooking completed, they removed the parcels, dried the cooked bulbs and roots and stored them in baskets. Later the cook needed only to soak the dried bulbs to serve them.

Baskets and Mats

Nisqually Indian baskets were made of the inner portions of cedar bark, small cedar roots, spruce roots, rushes, grasses and cattails. Maidenhair fern stems and cherry bark strips were used

for imbrication or decoration. All of these materials were found in the foothills of the mountain. The Nisqually women used two methods of weaving their baskets, coiling and twining. They made their baskets in various shapes and sizes, depending upon the use intended. The most popular were cooking baskets, berry baskets and storage baskets.

The cattail stalks and leaf blades were collected and dried during the summer months, as were the other baskets and mat-making materials. During the long winter months when family activities were carried on inside the big longhouse dwelling, the women would spend many hours at their craft. To ensure that the mats would lie flat, the cattails were folded and creased in a special way. They were then sewn together with a long nettle string and were made in many shapes and sizes, varying in thickness. Mats were used for tablecloths, floor and wall coverings, pillows and sleeping mats.

Plants used for herbal medicines were gathered and dried during berry-picking time. Almost every plant had curing qualities. Some were made into teas, others chewed or rubbed onto the body. Each village usually had a medicine or herbal woman who used her herbal knowledge to doctor the sick with her secret remedies. Her practice was most always passed on to one of her offspring. The herbal woman must not be confused with the "medicine man." She healed with herbs while he practiced spiritual healing.

Utilitarian Uses

The giant cedar trees were cut down by burning a ring of fire around the base of the tree, then chipping it with a cutting tool called an adze. When the tree was felled, it was cut into proper lengths for house planks, then split and adzed into the required shape. Each cedar dwelling house measured from 50 to 100 feet in length and was about 30 feet wide, the reason why these homes are sometimes called longhouses. Each house provided room for several families, each with a separate family fire and sleeping area. Bench-like beds were built along the outside walls with storage space underneath. Cattail mats adorned the walls to keep out the winter drafts. Each village contained from one to three houses, and the population was never allowed to become too large, mainly to ensure the safety of all of the group but also to control any outbreak of a deadly illness.

The cedar logs also were used for canoes. The log was cut to the proper length, shaped with an adze, then the inner section was cleaned out by alternate burning and chipping. The river canoe was called a shovel-nosed canoe because of its straight-lined ends and its flat bottom. Instead of paddles, the river canoe had poles that were used to push the canoe along in the shallow river water.

The soft inner bark of the cedar tree, pounded and softened, was used to fashion clothing. The women wore cedar-bark skirts, capes and conical basket-like hats. The men wore only a breech clout except in winter when they added shirts and leggings and when both sexes added fur undergarments for warmth. Cedar-bark clothing shed the rain, a quality that

70

gave it top priority. Moccasins were worn, but everyone went barefoot if the weather permitted.

Every utensil or tool was made from what nature provided– wood, bone or stone. There were no metal items introduced until trading began with the first foreign visitors. The Nisqually people had everything they needed.

Vision Quests

It was into the mountain foothills that the Nisqually youths went for their vision quests. It was the custom of the young people to seek a spirit partner when they were about 12 to 15 years of age. A youth prepared himself for this spirit quest through a rigorous period of training. He would go alone into the forest, find a clear stream and there make camp. He would bathe himself in the cool water, rub his body with certain herbs and keep himself in a receptive state of mind, waiting for a spirit power to come to him while he was in a trance or in a dreaming state. Once obtained, the spirit power would be his companion throughout his lifetime and would add its characteristics to those of the youth. Spirit powers included those of the wolf, the deer, the bear, the salmon, the hawk, the loon and so forth. Spirit powers could also be those of the natural elements such as the wind, the thunder and the like.

There are many other aspects of the traditional Nisqually Indian cultural life that are not covered here. There were certain ways of curing the sick, raising children, treating the elders of the village, playing games and traveling. If the reader wishes to explore further, there are other sources to consult.

Puget Sound Salish basketmaker, ca. 1900. Photo by Anders B. Wilse, University of Washington Libraries, Special Collections, MOHAI 88.33.115

Continued Use of the Natural Resources – *Chapter 13*

There were three time periods during which the natural resources of Mount Rainier were used by the Nisqually Indian people. The first was the traditional period as described in the preceding chapter, the time before the Medicine Creek Treaty was negotiated between the United States and the lower Puget Sound tribes on December 26, 1854. During this period the Nisqually Indian people who lived in the Nisqually River watershed roamed the foothills of the mountain to hunt deer and to gather berries and basket material.

The second period began after the Indian War of 1855-56 when the Nisqually Indian Reservation was established and all of the Nisqually people were expected to move onto the land located on the lower segment of the Nisqually River, about four miles from the river delta. Some of the members of the Squaitz village on Skate Creek, however, did not relocate but remained in their mountain home. They were joined in 1864 by So-to-lic, also known as Indian Henry, a Yakima Indian, who took up residence on the Mashel Prairie, and who selected each of his three wives from the Squaitz village. So-to-lic created an Indian settlement on the Mashel which attracted other Indian families who chose not to move onto the reservation. During this period the mountain natural resources were used by the remnant of the Squaitz village, by Indian Henry and his followers and by many of the older families who now lived on the reservation.

The third period encompasses the last sixty years, after which the residents of the upper village had moved away or died and Indian Henry's settlement had become but a memory in the minds of the old timers of the town of Eatonville. The main user group now became the Indian people who lived on or near the Nisqually Reservation, who made their yearly trek to the mountain to pick the blue huckleberries and to gather the herbal plants. Occassionally a young person traveled mountainward to find an isolated place for his vision quest.

Perhaps the most remembered use of the mountain resources occurred during the time that Indian Henry and his followers lived on Mashel Prairie. From that period came the stories of his occasional treks to a particular meadow on the mountain slopes to hunt the deer and the mountain goat. Walking had for centuries been the mode of traveling for his ancestors, but just before Indian Henry's time the horse came into use, lifting a burden from the Indian's back as the packhorse carried the game down the mountainside.

During this period of time, the towns of Elbe and Eatonville were established as white settlers came to claim the woods and the prairies. With them came a written account of history, of Henry, and of his hunting parties going up the mountain. Because deer and elk could be hunted in the lowlands, it was the mountain goat that gained the limelight in those times.

It has been established that the mountain goats ranged on the high rugged crags and cliffs above the timberline. They were fleet of foot, so the ice fields and steep inclines posed no

problems for them. These goats fed on the higher grassy meadows in the summer and moved to the lower elevations in the winter. When the gun came into use and the Indian hunter no longer had to rely on his bow and arrow or his snares and pits, the mountain goat became an addition to the food supply. The meat would be eaten, the fur would be cured for bed blankets and the wool, gathered from where it snagged onto the mountain bushes, was woven into bed mats.

Mountain: An upward pointed triangle of solid color. A single or double row of these represents a mountain range.

From: Crow's Shells: Artistic Basketry of Puget Sound by Nile Thompson and Carolyn Marr

PART FIVE: Men of the Mountain

Paradise Canyon and the 150 ft. Sluiskin Falls, named after the Indian Guide, Sluiskin. Photo by A.H. Barnes, 1910. University of Washington Libraries, Special Collections, BARNES581

Early Indian Guides – *Chapter 14*

When the British and the Americans arrived in Nisqually country, the first thing they saw was the mountain. In 1792, Captain George Vancouver, a British explorer, had bestowed upon Ta-co-bet the name of Mount Rainier. Today, two hundred years later, the name remains.

When the newcomers first anticipated climbing to the summit of Mount Rainier, their initial thought was to ask a local Indian to guide them. Who would know the mountain slopes better than he would? To their amazement they found Indian guides not very anxious to accompany them. The guides would agree to go just so far up the mountainside and no further. The fear of going to the summit was very real. There were evil spirit forces up there in the sacred area and anyone daring to penetrate that area would be smitten dead. They would not go–their word was good, they would not go. Not one of the guides acknowledged in this narrative went beyond the invisible line where the spirits reigned supreme.

La-ha-let

The first to attempt to climb up the mountain slopes was Dr. William Tolmie in 1833. A young man, freshly arrived from England, Tolmie found himself with time to explore around and about Fort Nisqually, a British fur-trading fort located near the mouth of the Nisqually River. While waiting for a sailing vessel to take him to his new post in the northlands, he decided to "climb the mountain." He told the local Indian people that his sole purpose was to gather herbs for his medicinal herb collection. He called it a "botanizing excursion." He left Fort Nisqually on August 29, 1833, accompanied by five Indian men as follows:

> "We were six in number. I have engaged Lachalet [La-ha-let, a Nisqually] for a blanket and his nephew Lashima for ammunition to accompany me and Nuckalkat a Puyallup, with two horses to be guides on the mountain ...and Quilniash, his relative, a very active, strong fellow has volunteered to accompany us. The Indians are in great hopes of killing elk and cheurevil [deer] and Lachalet has already been selling and promising the grease he is to get. It is in a great measure the expectation of finding game that urges them to undertake the journey." (Tolmie: 1963, 230)

Tolmie's journey took him up the Puyallup River, crossing and recrossing the river several times. Penetrating dense woods, through patches of ferns and underbrush, the group plunged on, sometimes on horseback, other times by foot. They ate berries and dried meat. Torrents of rain often complicated the trip.

It is difficult to determine how far up the mountainside Tolmie had planned to go or how many of his assortment of guides would desert him if he went too far. Early on his journey Tolmie wrote in his journal, "Lachalet has tonight been trying to dissuade me from going to the snow on the mountain." But Tolmie did indeed reach the snowline where the snow was "ankle-deep." There he gathered a quality of plants, peered up at the peak of Mount Rainier, then turned to retrace his steps.

Had he continued on he would surely have been alone, as his Indian companions would have deserted him. Today a creek bearing Tolmie's name lies just northwest of Lake Eunice, and Tolmie Peak is situated due north of the lake, reminders of the first white man known to attempt to scale the slopes of Mount Rainier.

Pierre Charles

The next white person known to travel mountainward was an American, Lt. Robert Johnson, a member of the Wilke's Expedition. Johnson left Fort Nisqually on May 19, 1841 to lead an exploring party inland over the Naches Pass. Pierre Charles was their guide.

Pierre Charles was of Indian and French-Canadian ancestry. He was an employee of the Hudson's Bay Company and well known for his abilities as a guide and as a hunter. He guided the Johnson party across the mountain pass and far into eastern Washington. The group returned over Naches Pass and on July 15, 1841, reached Fort Nisqually, having completed a journey of over a thousand miles. (Meany: 1916, 33)

Loolowcan

One cannot omit the colorful character of Theodore Winthrop who also trekked across the mountain on one of its northern slopes. The year was 1853. Winthrop had arrived at Fort Nisqually from Fort Victoria on somewhat of a sight-seeing tour. An American and a writer, his accounts of whom

he met and what he did have lasted through the years, as did a Nisqually legend told to him by a Nisqually named Hamitchou. "The Legend of Mount Rainier," appears elsewhere in this book. It depicts the miser who climbed to the top of Ta-co-bet in search of great riches and who met numerous obstacles in his pursuit.

Winthrop's account of his travels over the mountain pass presented the name Tacoma as the Indian name of Mount Rainier. His guide was Loolowcan, son of Owhigh, a prominent Klickitat Indian. Winthrop noted that his fellow Indian travelers respected the higher mountain slopes where gifts of appeasement to the mountain spirits hung on the tree branches, left there by previous Indian travelers who wished a safe journey over the mountain pass.

Later Indian Guides – *Chapter 15*

The next group of mountain climbers chose to travel up the Nisqually side of Mount Rainier. By this time the non-Indian population had grown considerably to include the soldiers stationed at Fort Steilacoom, an American military fort established in 1848, as well as a large assortment of American settlers. The British were still in charge of Fort Nisqually, a post that had been established as a fur-gathering fort in 1833 but had turned to agriculture in 1839. Although the British-American boundary had been set at the 49th parallel in 1846, the British holdings and personnel were allowed to remain intact until the United States purchased their land improvements from them—which would not happen until 1869.

Why these next three climbers chose to ascend the Nisqually side is unknown, but this approach to the peak may have appeared more accessible.

Lt. A.V. Kautz and Wah-pow-e-ty

Lt. Kautz is credited as the first to attempt to climb to the top of Mount Rainier. It was in 1857 while he was a soldier stationed at Fort Steilacoom that the time was right. The military forces at Fort Steilacoom had been instrumental in keeping peace among the Indian population and the American settlers. With the Indian treaties and the Indian war behind him, Kautz felt that the lull in military duties presented the chance for him to go. When he had talked of climbing the mountain in the past, other soldiers offered to go with him, but when he set the date, all offers were off. He did, however, end up with four soldiers from his post, two to accompany him to the top, the other two to stay with the horses when they had to be left behind. An officer who happened to be visiting from Fort Bellingham, Dr. O. R. Craig, also agreed to go. Kautz later wrote in his diary:

> "Information leading to the mountain was exceedingly meager; no white man had ever been near it, and Indians were very superstitious and afraid of it. The southern slope seemed the least abrupt and in that direction I proposed to reach the mountain; but whether to keep the high ground, or follow some stream to its source, was a question. Leschi, chief of the Nesquallies, was at that time in the guardhouse awaiting his execution, and as I had greatly interested myself to save him from his fate, he volunteered the information that the valley of the Nesqually River was the best approach after getting above the falls. He had some hope that I would take him as a guide; but finding that out of the question he suggested Wa-pow-e-ty, an old Indian of the Nesqually Tribe, as knowing more about the Nesqually than any other of his people." (Meany: 1916, 75)

After leaving the fort on July 8, 1857, Kautz's party stopped at the Nisqually Indian Reservation to pick up Wah-pow-e-ty. Horses were taken as far as the Mashel River; two of the soldiers were left there to watch out for them.

The Nisqually Canyon lay above the Mashel. In order to skirt the canyon, the party traveled inland and overland through

84

dense forests and thick underbrush before again joining the Nisqually River, a pattern that was to be repeated several times as the group moved mountainward. A combination of fatigue and meager rations took its toll on all of the members. The doctor, unused to such strenuous exercise, resorted to hiring Wah-pow-e-ty, a much smaller man, to carry his pack as well as his own. Wah-pow-e-ty also saved the day when he brought in a deer to add to the food supply. As a guide, though, the Indian fell short. He admitted that he had not been this far up on the river since he was but a small boy. So a joint effort between the party and the guide was put into force, planning the route as they went.

A base camp was made at the snow line. On the seventh day of the trip, Kautz alone found himself on the highest portion of the mountain which he was to attain. With the food supply almost depleted, the decision not to try to climb further was made. Wah-pow-e-ty became snow-blind and had to be guided down the mountainside. The group returned to the fort "hungry, haggard and sunburnt," their clothes in rags. (Meany: 1916, 92-3)

The trip took its toll, the mountain collected its dues. At the end of the journey Kautz had lost 14 pounds; the doctor had lost 21 pounds; two of the soldiers reported to the post hospital; one of them, upon applying for his pension, reported he had never fully recovered from the mountain trip. Old Wah-pow-e-ty suffered from an attack of "gastritis and barely escaped with his life after a protracted sickness." This problem was added to his being snow-blinded for some time. The doctor suffered from violent stomach pains and did not recover for three months.

Kautz fared better, a condition he attributed to the "precautions I took in eating when satisfying the first cravings of hunger on our return to camp." (Meany: 1916, 93)

Hazard Stevens and Sluiskin

The first successful ascent of Mount Rainier was made in 1870 by General Hazard Stevens, son of the first territorial governor of Washington Territory. Stevens' account began:

> "Takhoma had never been ascended. It was a virgin peak. The superstitious fears and traditions of the Indians, as well as the dangers of the ascent, had prevented their attempting to reach the summit, and the failure of a gallant and energetic officer [Kautz] ... had in general estimation proved it insurmountable." (Meany: 1916, 96)

Surrounding himself with hardy men, Stevens left Olympia with Philomon Beecher Van Trump, a mine worker, and Edward T. Coleman, an experienced mountain climber. The trio journeyed to the Yelm Prairie where they were joined by James Longmire who had agreed to guide them as far as Bear Prairie where an Indian guide could be obtained to take them the rest of the way.

Although Longmire had been in the area before with a surveying team, the trail he remembered had grown over and was difficult to find. In spite of the thick underbrush, crossing and recrossing the river and continually repacking loosened bundles that jiggled off of their horses, the group did reach Bear Prairie. There they stopped for a breather while Longmire took Stevens in search of Sluiskin, a Klickitat Indian who lived in the area.

Stevens wrote of meeting the Indian:

"Further search, however, was rewarded by the discovery of a rude shelter formed of a few skins thrown over a framework of poles, beneath which sat a squaw at work upon a half-dressed deerskin. An infant and a naked child of perhaps four years lay on the ground near the fire in front. Beside the lodge and quietly watching our approach, of which he alone seemed aware, stood a tall slender Indian clad in buckskin shirt and leggings, with a striped woolen breech-clout, and a single head garniture which gave him a single martial appearance. This consisted of an old military cap, the visor thickly studded with brassheaded nails, while a large circular brass article, which might have been the top of an oil-lamp, was fastened upon the crown. Several eagle feathers stuck in the crown and strips of fur sewed upon the sides completed the edifice, which, notwithstanding its components, appeared imposing rather than ridiculous. A long Hudson's Bay gun, the stock also ornamented with brass-headed tacks, lay in the hollow of the Indian's shoulder.

"He received us with great friendliness, yet not without dignity, shaking hands and motioning us to a seat beneath the rude shelter, while his squaw hastened to place before us suspicious-looking cakes of dried berries, apparently their only food." (Meany: 1917, 107)

Longmire made his request known to the Indian guide. Sluiskin agreed to meet the climbing party the next day at their Bear Prairie camp. There Sluiskin told Stevens that he had often hunted the mountain goat on the higher slopes but that he had never gone to the summit of the mountain. He quickly dismissed the group's idea that they would climb to the very top. Speaking in the Chinook jargon of that time, he described the route they should take:

> "Pointing to the almost perpendicular height immediately back or east of camp, towering three thousand feet or more overhead, loftiest mountain in sight, 'we go to the top of that mountain,' said he, 'and tomorrow we follow along the high backbone ridge of the mountains, now up, now down, first on one side then on the other, a long day's journey, and at last descending far down from the mountains into a deep valley, reach the base of Takhoma.'" (Meany: 1916, 108)

Longmire left to return home, taking his two mules and leaving a packhorse for the Steven's party return trip. The climbers pared down their loads to only the bare essentials, hiding the rest under a log.

The first day up the mountainside Coleman lagged behind the others. Sluiskin was sent back to locate him when it was discovered that he was out of sight. The Indian guide reported that Coleman had returned to the Bear Prairie camp. For three days the rest of the party trudged on, climbing over a most rugged route. Stevens noted:

> "...after climbing for hours an almost perpendicular peak—creeping on hands and knees over loose rocks, and clinging to scanty tufts of grass where a single slip would have sent us rolling a thousand feet down to destruction—we

reached the highest crest.... Directly in front...although twenty miles, old Takhoma loomed up more gigantic than ever.... On every side we looked down vertically thousands of feet, deep down into vast, terrible defiles, black and fir clothed, which stretched away until lost in the distance..." (Meany: 1916, 111)

When they came within a day's distance from the summit, Sluiskin began to voice his objection to continuing up the mountainside. Stevens wrote:

"The Indian, when starting from Bear Prairie, had evidently deemed our intention of ascending Takhoma too absurd to deserve notice. The turning back of Mr. Coleman only deepened his contempt for our prowess. But his views had undergone a change with the day's march. The affair began to look serious to him, and now in Chinook, interspersed with a few words of broken English and many signs and gesticulations, he began a solemn exhortation and warning against our rash project.

"Takhoma, he said, was an enchanted mountain, inhabited by an evil spirit, who dwelt in a fiery lake on its summit. No human being could ascend it or even attempt its ascent, and survive. At first, indeed the way was easy. The broad snow-fields over which he so often hunted the mountain goat, interposed no obstacle, but above them the rash adventurer would be compelled to climb up the steeps of loose rolling rocks, which would turn beneath his feet and cast him headlong into the deep abyss below. The upper snowslopes, too, were so steep that not even a goat, far less a man, could get over them. And he would have to pass below lofty walls and precipices whence avalanches of snow and vast masses of rocks were continually falling; and these would inevitably bury the intruder beneath their ruins. Moreover, a furious tempest continually swept the crown of the mountain, and the luckless adventurer, even if he wonderfully escaped the perils below, would be torn from the mountain and whirled through the air by this fearful blast. And the awful being upon the summit, who would surely punish the sacreligious attempt to invade his sanctuary,– who would hope to escape his vengeance? Many years ago, he continued, his grandfather, a great chief and warrior, and a mighty hunter, had ascended part way up the mountain, and had encountered some of these dangers, but he fortunately turned back in time to escape destruction, and no other had ever gone so far." (Meany: 1916, 114-5)

As Stevens and Van Trump planned their final ascent to the top of the mountain, Sluiskin requested a letter absolving him of any blame should the men perish on the mountain. Sluiskin said he would wait for them three days, then leave.

The two men left Sluiskin at the camp and traveled upward over a very precipitous route. At the end of the second day they planted a flag on a peak which they named Peak Success. The date was August 17, 1870. Noticing a slightly higher peak about a mile ahead of them, they continued on to a point today known as Columbia Crest to find jets of sulfur steam and smoke issuing out of a circular crater. They spent their second night on the mountain in an ice cave. Marking the spot with a brass plate inscribed with their names, they began their descent down the steep slopes among the rolling rocks and melting ice. As they neared the camp where they had left their guide, Van Trump fell 40 feet down an incline, landing among loose rocks. Severely bruised and with a gash in his thigh, he was just able to make it into camp.

Needless to say, Sluiskin thought he was seeing ghosts as the two hobbled into camp. He had planned on leaving the next morning to report their demise. Stevens and Sluiskin took a "short cut" back to Bear Prairie and the guide was sent back with the packhorse to bring the injured Van Trump down. By using the shortcut, Stevens realized that Sluiskin had, indeed, taken them up a roundabout way in the hopes of discouraging the climb. And so ended another mountain climbing expedition.

George Bailey and So-to-lic

No book would be complete without an accounting of So-to-lic, or Indian Henry as he was more often called. Indian Henry took up residence on the Mashel Prairie in 1864. It was said that he left his Yakima village at Simco after an argument with his people and chose to cross the mountain to make a new life for himself. He most likely picked the Mashel Prairie because he had probably visited there before the Indian War of 1855-56 and knew that the people of the Mashel village had moved onto the Nisqually Indian Reservation. There were still a few residents at the Squaitz village, and from that village he chose his wives. He was said to have gotten on well with the white settlers who established themselves on nearby lands. He attracted other Indian families who, like himself, had chosen not to go onto a reservation. It was not long before a sizable Indian settlement had formed on the Mashel Prairie.

Although there are many stories about Indian Henry, this narrative will include only his adventure when he served as a guide for the George Bailey party who scaled Mount Rainier in 1884. The climbing party consisted of George Bailey, Philomon Beecher Van Trump and A. C. Ewing. Bailey met first with Van Trump, who had been to the mountaintop in 1870, and together they visited James Longmire and talked him into accompanying them. Ewing was known only as a native of Ohio. The group began their trip from Longmire's place on Yelm Prairie and traveled up the trails following the Nisqually River upstream and made their appearance at Indian Henry's abode on Mashel prairie. They asked Indian Henry if he would guide them up the mountain. The Indian agreed to go, but only as far as the horses would go, no further. Bailey wrote of his guide:

> "...terminating abruptly at Mishawl Prairie, where we passed the night, the welcome guests of Henry, a Klickitat [Yakima] Indian who had renounced allegiance to his tribe, adopted the dress and manners of living of the whites, married three buxom squaws, and settled down as a prosperous farmer. He had preempted a quarter section of land, fenced it, erected several good log buildings, and planted his land to wheat and vegetables, which appeared as thrifty and prosperous as any of the farms of the white settlers we had seen. Henry was skilled in woodcraft, and we needed his services to guide us to the mountain. For the moderate consideration of two dollars a day, he agreed to take us by the most direct route to the highest point that

could be reached by horses, there to remain in charge of the animals while we went forward on foot. The negotiation was carried on in Chinook by Longmire, whose long residence among the Indians had given him great fluency in the strange jargon, and the eloquent gestures and contortions so essential to its interpretations. Henry knew of the circuitous route that General Stevens had followed, and was confident he could take us by a way thirty miles shorter. Of this Longmire expressed doubts, but all agreed to follow our guide until we were convinced that he was in error." (Bailey: 1886, 269)

The party took the Nisqually Canyon bypass route up and over the Mashel River and through the thick underbrush. The trail came out near the present town of Elbe. The horses were constantly being tormented by yellowjackets, and the men were being eaten alive by gnats and mosquitoes. As the horses passed through the underbrush, they would walk into the bees' nest and the angry insects would sting the horses. In panic, the horses kicked up their heels, threw off their packs and ran helter-skelter. Relief came only when the party reached the colder atmosphere.

Besides the yellowjackets, mosquitoes and gnats, the party experienced difficulties in moving through the thick underbrush with fallen trees lying across their paths. Getting a horse over such hurdles was no easy matter. In crossing and recrossing the river, both men and beasts were confronted with losing their balance on the slippery rocks and falling into the rushing river waters. If the lower trail presented such obstacles, what would the upper mountain trail be like?

Arriving at the snowline they made their last camp before ascending the mountain. Indian Henry and the horses would remain here. Bailey noticed Indian Henry's depression at this point as he wrote:

> "Henry who had not spoken a word the entire day and had looked as blue as possible, here made a last persuasive appeal to Longmire not to persist in his foolish attempt to scale the mountain. For the rest of us he did not seem to care, but on Longmire, as an old friend and neighbor, he wasted quite an amount of Chinook eloquence to save him from what he considered certain death. He said we would never get back alive if we succeeded in reaching the top; while if we were permitted to go part way by the spirit who dwelt at the summit, we would return maimed for life. He doubtless felt as he spoke, and departed from us in a dejected frame of mind as he turned to go back with the horses." (Bailey: 1886, 272)

Three of the four did go to the summit. Ewing, the lone dissenter, did not make the last day's climb. Upon return to the snowline camp, the climbers found it deserted. Bailey explained:

> "An unbroken stillness and solitude reigned in camp. Neither Henry or the horse could be seen or heard. The tent we found more carefully stretched than when the party left it, a trench had been dug about it, the provisions and camp equipage had been piled and covered in the center of the tent, and at either end a scarecrow, or rather scare wolf, had been improvised–the large fresh tracks of a wolf had been noticed on the snow not far from the camp. All

these preparations indicated the Indian had made a move-
ment not on the programme of the white man. Later in the
evening, after much whooping and several revolver shots
by one of the party, who had gone some distance down
the slope, Henry made his appearance and proceeded to
explain–with a preliminary ejaculation of his relief from a
grave responsibility. He concluded that the party had been
lost on the mountain, and he had put their house (tent) in
order, removed the horses to good pasturage below, had
moved his 'ictas' (personal effects) to that point, provided
himself with a few days rations, and on the morrow had
intended to start for home, to relate to their friends the supposed tragic fate of the mountaineers. It had been sad and
mournful business for him, but his joy at our return was as
genuine as his surprise, and we doubted if he really believed
that we had reached the top at all." (Bailey: 1886, 277)

Reminders of the Bailey Expedition remain not so much in the
names of the upper slopes to mark the event, but in something
that happened to one of their party. The story goes that James
Longmire discovered the mineral springs in the meadow where
the party had left their horses. (Grater: 74) Longmire later developed the area around the springs that today bear his name.

The names of the three Indian guides have been given to certain places on the mountain and remain today to honor these
men. They include Wapowety Cleaver, a high rocky ridge
overlooking the Kautz Glacier; Sluiskin Falls and Sluiskin
Mountain; and Indian Henry's Hunting Ground.

Fish Net: Intersecting diagonal lines form diamond-shaped spaces over the entire background of the basket. Found among the Twana, Skagit, Suquamish and Nisqually.

From: *Crow's Shells: Artistic Basketry of Puget Sound by Nile Thompson and Carolyn Marr*

# PART SIX:

Closing Remarks

Nisqually Glacier as viewed from the slope just west of Camp Reese. Photo by A.H. Barnes, 1910. University of Washington Libraries Special Collections, BARNES533

Should the Name be Ta-co-bet, Ta-ho-ma, or Rainier? – *Chapter 16*

The tallest peak of the Cascade Mountain Range, standing 14,410 feet above sea level, had been named long before Captain George Vancouver of the British Royal Navy bestowed upon it a second name in 1792–Mount Rainier. The Nisqually Indian name for the mountain was Ta-co-bet meaning " nourishing breasts" and/or "the place where the waters begin." The Yakima Indian people who lived east of the mountain called it Ta-ho-ma which literally meant the same as the Nisqually Indian name. Indian people tended to name a place to signify a distinguishing geographic feature.

As with every Indian word in those days when the British first came to Nisqually country to build a fur-gathering fort, there were several ways to spell a word. Indian people did not have a written language, only an oral language. So when one was asked the name of the mountain, the Indian would say it and the recorder of names would write it down phonetically, or as it sounded to him. Because there was a guttural sound within the name, the pronunciations could have been as varied as the recorded word. The early historians copied the Nisqually name for the mountain in these ways: Ta-co-bet, Ta-co-bed, Ta-cob and Ta-co-ma.

Dr. William Tolmie believed the Indian name for the mountain was Tuc-ho-ma back in 1833 when he took his trip to the mountain slopes on the Puyallup side to gather medicinal plants.

Later, in 1853, Theodore Winthrop, in telling the legend of the miser, recounted the name as Ta-co-ma. Lt. Kautz, in 1857, referred to the mountain as Takhoma. In 1869, the new settlement on Commencement Bay took the name of Tacoma and the popular name for the mountain became Tahoma.

In an attempt to legally change the name of the mountain from Mount Rainier to Mount Tahoma, Judge James Wickersham, a scholar of Nisqually Indian history, conducted research and collected a vast amount of information regarding the Indian name. On February 6, 1893, he presented his case before the Tacoma Academy of Science. When he had finished his discourse, there was no doubt but that the Nisquallies called the mountain by the name of Ta-co-bet and the Yakimas called it by the name of Ta-ho-ma and the citizens of Tacoma favored bestowing the name of Tacoma on the mountain peak called Mount Rainier.

Even though the Northern Pacific Railroad had announced its intention of adopting the name Mount Tahoma in its advertising campaign, the United States Board of Geographic Names voted in 1890 to retain the name of Mount Rainier. When the United States Congress voted on March 2, 1889, to create a national park around the mountain, they more or less decided the name issue for good by establishing the Mount Rainier National Park.

Despite the national opposition, the people of Pierce County have continued to carry the banner supporting the name of Tahoma for the mountain. In 1917 and again in 1924 the board was asked to consider the name change. The answer was no. For

many years publications listing Mount Rainier carried the name
of Mount Tahoma in parentheses beside it.

When the Washington State Board for Geographic Names was
formed, it was approached to consider the Indian name for the
mountain, most recently in 1978 and 1983. The answer was always no, no and no—Mount Rainier it is, it was said, and Mount
Rainier it will continue to be!

All those who continue to wish the mountain carried the name
of Mount Tahoma will have to find solace in the fact that for
most of the Indian people of the lower Puget Sound the mountain has always been and always will be Mount Tahoma. And
to the people of the Nisqually Indian Tribe it has always been
their Ta-co-bet, the place where the waters begin.

Ta-co-bet, Majestic Mountain, Silhouetted against our eastern sky
Guardian over the land of the Nisqually people
Who sends the rains to renew our spirits
Who feeds the river, the home of our salmon,
Who protects our eagle in her flight,
Who reaches upward through the floating clouds
To touch the hand of the Great Spirit.
Ta-co-bet
We honor you
The People of the Nisqually Indian Tribe

This text by Cecilia Svinth Carpenter originally appeared on the panel of a monument at LaGrande Dam honoring the mountain and it's relationship to the people. "Mount Rainier from above Myrtle Falls in August," photo courtesy Samuel Kerr. ⓒ

In Closing – *Chapter 17*

E legant, and majestic, the mountain still stands, filling the eastern sky above Nisqually country, keeping watch over the Indian dwelling places and fishing weirs, filling the river with life-sustaining water, and causing the gentle rains to fall on the lands.

Clothed in her robes of glistening white, Ta-co-bet, the mountain, has kept faith with the traditional Nisqually Indian people whose descendants continue to offer up their songs of thankfulness, praise and adoration.

Nisqually families, today, go each summer to the lower slopes of Ta-co-bet to pick the blue huckleberries and search for herbal plants. There are no attempts to climb to the upper slopes above the sacred line to compete with the strength of the mountain spirits who continue to guard the hallowed ground created by the Great Mystery.

Today the land and the mountain are shared with those who came here over a hundred years ago to build cement cities and highways. No longer does the mountain belong solely to the Indian people who easily recognize that for every beneficent feature of Ta-co-bet there lies an equally evil force awaiting those who dare to trespass above the sacred demarcation line. Each time the newspaper headlines carry the news that another person has died on the upper mountain slopes, they know that the spirit forces of the mountain have claimed another life, and the Indian residents of Nisqually country sigh and shed a tear within for those who would not heed the laws of the mountain. The spirits who live on the mountain will always have the last word.

Icicle: A downward pointed triangle of solid color.

From: Crow's Shells: Artistic Basketry of Puget Sound by Nile Thompson and Carolyn Marr

Bibliography

Bagley, Clarence B. *Indian Myths of the Northwest*. Seattle: Lowman and Hanford Company, 1930.

Bailey, George. "Ascent of Mount Rainier," *The Overland Monthly*. San Francisco: 1886, pp. 266-278. Volume 7.

Brockman, C. Frank. *Flora of Mount Rainier National Park*. Washington D.C.: Government Printing Office, 1947.

Carpenter, Cecelia Svinth. *Fort Nisqually, A Documented History of Indian and British Interaction*. Tacoma: Tahoma Research Service, 1986.

Carpenter, Cecelia Svinth. "Historic Perspectives of the Nisqually Tribal Resources." Olympia: The Nisqually Indian Tribe, 1986.

Carpenter, Cecelia Svinth. *They Walked Before: Indians of Washington State*. Tacoma: A Bicentennial Publication, Washington State Historical Society, 1977.

Clark, Ella E. *Indian Legends of the Pacific Northwest*. Los Angeles: University of California Press, 1953.

Eells, Myron. "Aboriginal Geographic Names." *American Anthropologist*. January 1892.

Gibbs, George. "Map of the Western District of Washington Territory Showing the Position of the Indian Tribes and the Land Ceded by the Treaty." 1855.

Gibbs, George. *Northwestern Mythology*. Bureau of American Ethnology, #3438, 1856.

Grater, Russell K. *Grater's Guide to Mount Rainier National Park*. Portland: Binsford and Mort, publication year unknown.

Gunther, Erna. *Ethnobotany of Western Washington*. Seattle: University of Washington Press, 1973.

Haeberlin, Hermann and Erna Gunther. *The Indians of Puget Sound*. Seattle: University of Washington, 1930.

Hlavin, Jeanette and Pearl Engal. *History of Tacoma Eastern Area*. Unpublished manuscript.

Lane, Barbara. *"History of the Nisqually Indian Use of the Upper Portion of the Nisqually River and Tributary Creeks."* Olympia: Nisqually Indian Tribe, 1977.

Longmire, Elcaine. "A Biographical Sketch." An unpublished paper. Circa 1910.

Loutzenhiser, Floss H. "Indian Legends Have Changed Over the Years." A newspaper article, name and date unknown.

Lymon, W.D. "Rainier Indian Legends." *Washington Magazine*. August 1906, pp. 449-452.

Meany, Edmond S. *Mount Rainier, A Record of Exploration*. Portland: Binsford and Mort, 1916.

Smith, Marian W. *The Puyallup-Nisqually*. Seattle: University of Washington Press, 1940. Reprinted in 1969 by AMS Press.

Spier, Leslie. "Tribal Distributions in Washington." *General Series in Anthropology*. Number 3, Menasha, Wisconsin: George Banta Publishing Company, 1936.

Stevens, Hazard. "The First Ascent of Takhoma." *The Atlanta Monthly*. Volume 38, November 1876. Reprint by Shorey Publications.

Swanton, John R. *Indian Tribes of the Pacific Northwest*. Shorey Reprint, 1974.

Tacoma News Tribune articles: March 21, 1979; July 5, 1975; November 28, 1977; concerning the Sasquatch.

"Take a Clear Breath, Clear Throat, Say Ohanapecosh." Seattle: University of Washington, *Dunbar Scrapbook*, newspaper article, date unknown.

Tolmie, William F. *The Journals of William Fraser Tolmie, Physician and Fur Trader*. Vancouver, B.C.: Mitchell Press, 1963.

U.S. Department of the Interior. *The Encyclopedia of Information of Mount Rainier. Volume Two, Part One.*

Walker, R. "Sketch of the Western Approach to the Cowlitz Pass." Map, 1878.

Wickersham, James. "Is It Mount Tacoma or Rainier?" Tacoma: News Publishing Company, 1893.

Wickersham, James. "Nusqually Mythology." *Overland Monthly*. October 1898, pp. 346-351.

Winthrop, Theodore. *Canoe and Saddle*. Boston: Tickner and Fields, 1863. Later published by Binford and Mort of Portland, Oregon.

CPSIA information can be obtained
at www.ICGtesting.com
Printed in the USA
BVHW01s0304281217
503693BV00002B/146/P